© 1991 The Walt Disney Company

No portion of this book may be reproduced
without the written consent of The Walt Disney Company.

Produced by Kroha Associates, Inc.
Middletown, Connecticut.

Illustrated by Alvin S. White Studio
Burbank, California.

Printed in the United States of America.

ISBN 1-56326-013-1

Snack Surprises

Today at preschool, the Disney Babies are going to have a special treat at snack time. Their teacher says the treat is a surprise! The Disney Babies can't wait! They wash their hands and sit down at the table.

Baby Goofy tucks his napkin under his chin. The napkin will keep his shirt clean. Baby Clarabelle and Baby Donald tuck in their napkins too.

The teacher gives each Disney Baby a paper
cup. Then she fills each cup with juice.

Baby Donald loves juice. He starts to drink his right away.

"Wait!" says Baby Goofy. He wants Baby Donald to save some juice to drink with the snack.

The Disney Babies wonder what the teacher will
bring them. They close their eyes and think of all
their favorite treats. Then each Disney Baby tries to
guess what the snack surprise will be.

   Baby Clarabelle guesses that the snack surprise
will be cookies. Baby Clarabelle likes cookies more
than any other dessert.
   "No, it is not cookies," says the teacher. "But it
is yummy."

Baby Goofy guesses that the surprise will be ice cream. He likes ice cream, especially ice-cream sundaes. "No," says the teacher. "But the surprise is as much fun to eat as a sundae."

Baby Donald guesses that the surprise will be candy. He likes all kinds of candy!

"No," says the teacher. "The surprise tastes sweet, but it is much better for you than candy."

No one guesses what the surprise is. It is not
cookies or candy or ice cream. What can it be?
"Your snack is almost ready!" says the teacher.

The Disney Babies look at their teacher. They try to see what she is making.

"Today's snack surprise is fruit — special fruit and yogurt!" she says.

Uh-oh! The Disney Babies are very disappointed.
Baby Clarabelle does not think fruit is as special as
cookies. She does not know what yogurt is, and
she does not want to try it!

Baby Donald does not think that fruit and yogurt
can taste as good as candy. And Baby Goofy is
sure that the snack surprise is not as much fun to
eat as ice cream!

"Who wants to try their snack surprise first?" asks the teacher.

The Disney Babies are quiet. They do not want to try the snack surprise. They want cookies or candy or ice cream.

Finally, Baby Goofy decides to try the snack surprise. Maybe he will like it. "Me!" says Baby Goofy.

The teacher gives Baby Goofy his snack surprise.
It is a boat made from a banana. A slice of
watermelon is the sail, and a piece of pineapple
is the flag!

There are even ocean waves made of yogurt and blueberries around the boat. The Disney Babies can't believe their eyes. The snack surprise looks delicious. It looks like it will be fun to eat too!

"Yummy!" says Baby Goofy. It is better than the sundae he imagined. He is glad he tried the snack.

"Snack, please!" says Baby Clarabelle.
"Me too?" asks Baby Donald.
The teacher gives a fruit boat to Baby Clarabelle
and another one to Baby Donald.

Today the Disney Babies tried something new.
They did not think the teacher's snack surprise
would taste good. But Baby Goofy helped them
discover a delicious treat.

The fruit boats their teacher made are more
special than cookies. They taste better than candy.
And they are more fun to eat than ice cream!
    "Our favorite!" agree all of the Disney Babies.

Parenting Matters

Dear Parent,

All too often children think that treats must be sugary and sweet to be good. But, in fact, healthful, nutritious foods can be just as tasty and as much fun to eat as sweets that are high in calories and low in nutrition.

In *Snack Surprises*, the *Disney Babies* are disappointed when their teacher does not surprise them with cookies, candy, or ice cream at snack time. Baby Goofy decides to be adventuresome and try the fruit snack offered by the teacher. Not only is the snack healthful, but it looks delightful and tastes delicious.

Snack Surprises helps young children know that:
- fruits are good-tasting and a better choice for snacks than sugary treats such as cookies and candy.
- the best way to discover new foods is to taste them.
- unfamiliar foods can be just as tasty as foods they are accustomed to eating.

Some Hints for Parents
- Presenting and arranging meals and snacks in fun ways may help young children try new foods.
- Keep fresh fruits, yogurt, and non-sugary cereals on hand for treats.
- Praise children for trying new foods.
- Point out different fruits and vegetables at the grocery store, and encourage children to try new foods.